Tom and Ricky

and the

Chocolate Machine Mystery

Bob Wright

High Noon Books
Novato, California

Cover Design: Nancy Peach
Interior Illustrations: Herb Heidinger

Glossary: number, box, fence, plans

International Standard Book Number: 0-87879-365-8

10 09 08 07
15 14 13 12 11

You'll enjoy all the High Noon Books. Write for
a free full list of titles.

Contents

CHAPTER 1

A Friend by the Fence

Patches was sitting in the yard. It was a hot day. Tom and Ricky were not there. They were fishing down at the creek.

All of a sudden Patches sat up. He could hear something. He didn't know what it was. He started to bark.

Then he saw another dog. It was sitting on the other side of the fence. Patches barked again. Then he wagged his tail. The other dog didn't do anything. It just sat there.

1

Patches ran to the fence. The other dog was big. It was hurt. It had a bad cut on its leg. It was all dirty. It wanted to come into the yard with Patches.

Patches started to dig a hole. It was too small. The other dog couldn't get into it.

Then Patches ran to the house. No one was there. He ran back to the fence. The other dog just sat by the fence.

Then Patches heard Tom and Ricky. He barked and barked.

"Patches, what is it?" Tom said.

Patches ran to him and Ricky. Then he ran back to the fence. He kept barking.

"What do you want?" Tom asked.

Tom went over to the fence. Ricky took the fish into the house. Then he came back out.

"Ricky, come here," Tom called out.

"Ricky, come here," Tom called out.

"What's up? What's going on?" Ricky asked.

"Come over here. Look at this dog. He's hurt. Look at his leg. He has a bad cut," Tom said.

"Now I know why Patches was barking," Ricky said.

"I think we can help him," Tom said.

"How?" Ricky asked.

"Let's carry him into your yard," Tom said.

"He's a big dog. But let's try," Ricky said.

Tom and Ricky got over the fence. The big dog didn't move. It just looked at them. It was hard for him to walk or move.

"Let's both get him," Tom said.

"Don't worry, boy. We'll help you," Ricky said.

They both got the dog. It was hard. But they got him into Ricky's yard.

Ricky's mother was home by now. She came into the yard. "What do you have there?" she asked.

"Patches saw this dog. He must know him. He was barking and barking. Tom and I got the dog into the yard," Ricky said.

"That dog is hurt," she said.

"What should we do?" Tom asked.

"I see a dog tag. His name is Bandit. The tag says to call 555-3840. Ricky, call that number. Let them know that Bandit is here," she said.

CHAPTER 2

The Man Who Yells

Ricky called the number. Then he went back into the yard. His mother and Tom were with Bandit.

"No one is home at that number," Ricky said.

"Well, I think we should clean Bandit up," Ricky's mother said.

She got some water and some rags. Tom and Ricky started to clean Bandit.

"This is a bad cut. But I think we can help him," she said.

"Bandit seems like a good dog," Ricky said.

"He sure does. You dry him off. Then I'll put a rag over that cut," she said.

"I bet he wants some food," Tom said.

Ricky ran in the house. Patches went in with him. Ricky got some food and water. He took it out to Bandit. But Bandit didn't eat any of it. He just looked at it.

Then Patches started to eat some of the food. Bandit saw Patches eating. He got up and went over to the food.

"Look! Now he's eating, too," Tom said.

"He did want some food after all," Ricky's mother said.

"Now what do we do?" Tom asked.

"You know what? I'm going to call Mr. Jones, the vet. He knows almost all the dogs in town. He might know who Bandit belongs to," Ricky's mother said. Then she went into the house.

"I sure hope your mother can find out where Bandit lives," Tom said.

"I do, too," Ricky said.

Ricky's mother came back out of the house. "Mr. Jones says the dog might belong to Mr. Lake. I know where he lives. It's near Front Street. Come on. Let's all go over there," she said.

"How do you know where Mr. Lake lives?" Ricky asked.

"A lot of people know Mr. Lake. He likes to make things," she answered.

Patches jumped up. "No, Patches. You and Bandit stay here. We'll be right back," Ricky said.

They all got into the car.

"How do you think Bandit got hurt?" Tom asked.

"Maybe he got hit by a car," Ricky answered.

By now they were at Mr. Lake's house.

"Go up and ask Mr. Lake if his dog is there," Ricky's mother said.

Tom and Ricky got out of the car. They went up to Mr. Lake's house.

A big man came out of the house.

"What do you want?" he yelled at them.

"Are you Mr. Lake?" Ricky asked.

A big man came out of the house.

"What's it to you?" the man yelled back.

"We're just looking for Mr. Lake," Tom said.

"Well, he isn't here. Now get out of here," the man yelled.

Tom and Ricky went back to the car.

"What was that all about?" Ricky's mother asked.

"That big man told us to go away," Tom said.

"Did you ask him about Bandit?" she asked.

"We couldn't," Ricky said.

"Well, just go back and ask if Bandit lives there," she said.

"OK. If you say so," Ricky said.

This time Ricky went alone. The same man saw him.

"Didn't I tell you to get out of here?" the man said.

"Do you have a dog named Bandit?" Ricky asked.

"Bandit? Bandit? Where's that dog?" the man asked.

Ricky didn't say anything. He looked in the house in back of the man. He saw another man sitting down. The other man had white hair. He was old. He looked hurt.

The man at the door looked at Ricky. Then he yelled, "I'll go get him. No, I can't go. You bring me that dog. Bring him here."

"OK. OK," Ricky said. He went back to the car.

"How did it go?" Tom asked.

"That big man said to bring Bandit here. But I saw another man in the house. He is old and small and has white hair," Ricky said.

"That's Mr. Lake," Ricky's mother said.

"Who's the man who was yelling?" Tom asked.

"I don't know. But if that's Bandit's home, we have to bring him here," she said.

"Poor Bandit. I hope he will be all right," Ricky said.

Then they all started back to Ricky's house to get Bandit.

CHAPTER 3

The Black Box

Tom and Ricky were talking all the way back home. They didn't like that man.

"Who could that man be?" Ricky asked.

"I don't know," his mother answered.

"I sure didn't like him," Ricky said.

"Do you know Mr. Lake?" Tom asked.

"No, I don't. I have heard a lot about him. He is always making things," Ricky's mother said.

"Like what?" Ricky asked.

"Well, I heard that he was working on a new chocolate machine, she answered.

"A chocolate machine?" Tom said.

"That's what I heard," she answered.

"Tell us about it," Ricky said.

"Mr. Lake has plans for a machine that will make chocolate in five minutes," she said.

"Five minutes?" Tom asked.

"That's right. Chocolate takes a long time to make. But his machine will do it in five minutes," she said.

"Has he made the machine? I'd sure like to see it," Ricky said.

"I heard that he just had the plans. He hasn't made the machine yet," she said.

"I'll bet he will make a lot of chocolate with that machine," Tom said.

"And a lot of money, too," Ricky said.

"Well, here we are, back home," Ricky's mother said.

Tom and Ricky jumped out of the car. They ran into the yard.

"Come here, Patches. Come on, Bandit," Ricky called out.

"I don't see them anywhere," Tom said.

"Maybe they went for a walk. Maybe Bandit went home," Ricky said.

Then Ricky's mother called, "Where did these fish come from?"

"From the creek," Ricky answered.

"Well, come on in and clean them," she called back.

They started to go in. Then they heard Patches barking.

"Look! There's Patches. And Bandit is with him," Tom said.

"Bandit has something. It looks like a black box," Ricky said.

Ricky's mother looked at Patches and Bandit. "They are all dirty. Where have they been?" she asked.

"They might have dug up that box," Tom said.

"Do you think there is anything in that box?" she asked.

"Let's find out. Come here, Bandit. Nice Bandit. I won't hurt you," Ricky said.

Bandit went over to Ricky. He dropped the black box in front of him.

"Nice Bandit," Ricky said.

The black box was all dirty. Ricky rubbed off the dirt. The box said, "E.L. Lake" on the top.

"This box is Mr. Lake's," Ricky said.

Bandit barked. He seemed to know what Ricky was saying.

"Open it up," Tom said.

Ricky opened it up. There were many papers in it. "What could all this be?" Ricky asked.

"Let me see them," Tom said.

"I think I hear your dad. He just got home from work," Ricky's mother said.

Ricky's dad came into the yard. Tom and Ricky told him about Bandit. They told him about going to Mr. Lake's house. Then they told him that Bandit and Patches had the black box.

"Let me see the papers," Ricky's dad said.

Ricky's dad looked at them for a long time. Then he said, "The papers say 'The Chocolate Machine Plans—E.L. Lake.' What's this all about?"

"Those must be the plans for Mr. Lake's Chocolate Machine!" Ricky said.

CHAPTER 4

The Chocolate Machine

Ricky's dad looked at the plans for the Chocolate Machine. Then he looked back at Tom and Ricky. "There's something funny about all of this," he said.

"Do you think we should take Bandit back to his home?" Tom asked.

"No. I don't like any of this. Why was Bandit hurt? Who is that man at Mr. Lake's house? Why did Bandit and Patches bring that black box to us?" Ricky's dad said.

"Do you think that Chocolate Machine will work?" Ricky asked his dad.

"It might," his dad answered.

Ricky's dad looked at the plans for the Chocolate Machine.

"What do you think?" Ricky asked his mother.

"Well, I don't know anything about machines. But Mr. Lake has made a lot of other machines. And all of them have worked," she said.

"If this machine works, Mr. Lake will make a lot of money. Every home could have one," Ricky's dad said.

"How about that! We could have our own Chocolate Machine!" Ricky said.

"A machine that makes chocolate in five minutes!" Ricky's dad said.

"How did the plans get in that box?" Tom asked.

"I bet Mr. Lake put them there. He wanted to hide them. He wanted to keep them safe," Ricky said.

"But how did Bandit get hurt?" Tom asked.

"And why were Patches and Bandit all dirty when they came home with the box?" Ricky asked.

"Stop. You're going too fast," Ricky's dad said.

"It just doesn't add up," Tom said.

"Something is wrong," Ricky said.

"Boys, I think someone wants those plans," Ricky's dad said.

"What do you mean? What's going on here?" Tom asked.

"I don't think that man you saw lives in this town. I think he heard about the Chocolate Machine. He might have come here to get those plans," Ricky's dad said.

"Maybe Bandit hid the plans. He wanted to help Mr. Lake," Ricky said.

"I think you could be right," Ricky's dad said.

"Then that's why the man wants Bandit. I bet he knows that Bandit hid the plans," Tom said.

"Bandit wanted to help Mr. Lake," Ricky said.

"And Patches helped Bandit," Tom said.

Patches wagged his tail.

"Ricky, call Sergeant Collins. I think we better tell him what's going on," Ricky's dad said.

Then Ricky's mother called out, "What about these fish?"

"Later, Mom. I have to call Sergeant Collins right now," Ricky said.

CHAPTER 5

Sergeant Collins Helps Out

Ricky called Sergeant Collins. He got to Ricky's house very fast.

"I know Mr. Lake. He is a nice, old man. And I know Bandit. He is a good dog," the Sergeant said.

"What's going on?" Ricky asked.

"It doesn't look good to me. I don't like any of it," the Sergeant said.

"What do you think we should do?" Tom asked.

"I have an idea. It might work," Sergeant Collins said.

"What is it? We'll do anything to help Mr. Lake," Ricky said.

"Call Mr. Lake's house. Tell that man you have Bandit and a black box," Sergeant Collins said to Ricky.

"Tell him I have the black box?" Ricky said.

"That's right. Tell him you can't bring him the box or Bandit. Tell him he has to come here to get them," Sergeant Collins said.

"Do you think he will come here?" Ricky asked.

"I think he will. He wants that box with the plans," the Sergeant said.

"OK. Let's try it," Ricky said.

Ricky went to the phone. He called Mr. Lake's number. The man answered the phone.

"I came over today to see Mr. Lake," Ricky said.

"What do you want now? Where's that dog?" the man said.

"I have Bandit here with me. And I have a dirty black box. I didn't know what to do with it," Ricky said.

"A black box! Did you open it?" the man asked.

"Yes. There are some old papers in it. They have a lot of numbers on them. Do you know anything about it?" Ricky asked.

"Look, kid. I'm here helping Mr. Lake. He wants me to get that black box for him," the man said. He was trying to be nice.

"Sure, sure, I see," Ricky said.

"Well, you bring them to me right now. I'll give you $5.00 if you do," the man said.

"I can't go there. I'm all alone. I have to stay here at home. You come here," Ricky said.

"OK. OK. I'll be right there. Where do you live?" the man asked.

"932 Page Street. It's near Front Street," Ricky said.

"OK. OK. I'll find it." Then the man hung up.

"He's on his way," Ricky said.

"Good. We'll be ready for him," Sergeant Collins said.

"I have an idea," Tom said.

"What's that?" Ricky's dad asked.

"How about if I go over to Mr. Lake's house. I won't go in. I'll just see if Mr. Lake is alone. I'll see if he needs any help," Tom said.

"That's a good idea," Sergeant Collins said.

Tom got on his bike. He went as fast as he could. He saw the man go out of Mr. Lake's house. The man got in his car and left. Tom hid his bike. He walked to the house. He looked in. He saw Mr. Lake all tied up. He was all alone.

CHAPTER 6

Tom Helps Mr. Lake

Tom was sure Mr. Lake was all alone. He knew he had to help him. Maybe he could open the window. He pushed on it. It opened.

Mr. Lake saw Tom. "Who are you?" he called out.

"Do you need help, Mr. Lake?" Tom asked.

"Get these ropes off me," Mr. Lake said.

"Is anyone here with you?" Tom asked.

"No one is here. Just you and me. Come in and help me," Mr. Lake said.

Tom got in the house. He cut the ropes off Mr. Lake.

Mr. Lake looked happy.

Tom got in the house. He cut the ropes off Mr. Lake.

"I'm sure glad to see you. But who are you? How did you know I needed help? Where's Bandit?" Mr. Lake asked.

"Everything is OK. Bandit is safe. He's at Ricky's house," Tom said.

"Wno's Ricky?" Mr. Lake asked.

"I'll tell you all about it. Let me call Ricky and Sergeant Collins. I'll tell them you are all right," Tom said.

"I know Sergeant Collins. He's my friend," Mr. Lake said.

"He's our friend, too," Tom said.

Tom went to the phone. He called Ricky's house.

Ricky answered the phone.

"Ricky, is that man there yet?" Tom asked.

"He's parking in front of the house right now," Ricky said.

"I'm with Mr. Lake. I got in the house. We're all alone. He's safe now. He was all tied up but I got the ropes off," Tom said.

Sergeant Collins got on the phone. "Stay there, Tom. You'll be all right. That man is here. We'll take care of him."

"OK. We'll stay here. Come and get us as soon as you can," Tom said. Then he hung up.

The man got out of his big car. He walked up to Ricky's house.

Ricky opened the door.

The man just looked at him.

"OK, kid. Here's the $5.00. Now give me the black box. I'm in a hurry. Move fast," the man said.

"Come on in. I'll get the box and Bandit," Ricky said.

"I don't care about that dog. I just want the box," the man said.

The man walked into the house. Then he saw Sergeant Collins and Ricky's dad. "What's going on?" he said.

"That's what we want to know," Sergeant Collins said.

The man just looked at Sergeant Collins. Then he started to run.

Ricky moved out of the way.

Sergeant Collins jumped for him. He got him down. "I don't think you better move," Sergeant Collins said.

"OK. OK. I give up," the man said.

"I'm taking you in with me. I have a lot of things to ask you," Sergeant Collins said.

"I'll call Tom," Ricky said.

The man got up. He left with Sergeant Collins. "Let me know how Mr. Lake is," the Sergeant said.

"We will," Ricky's dad said.

Ricky got on the phone. "Tom, we're coming over. Sergeant Collins got that man. He's taking him in."

"Did everything go all right?" Tom asked.

"It sure did! You should have seen Sergeant Collins. He jumped right on the man. He got him down fast!" Ricky said.

"I'm sorry I missed that," Tom said.

"Stay right there. We'll be right over," Ricky said.

CHAPTER 7

The Mystery is Cleared Up

Ricky got in his dad's car. They took the black box. Patches jumped in with Bandit.

When Bandit saw the house, he started to bark. He jumped out as soon as Ricky's dad parked the car.

"I think Bandit is all right now," Ricky said.

"I think he's happy to be back home," Ricky's dad said.

They went up to the front door. Tom opened it for them.

Bandit ran in and jumped on Mr. Lake.

"Good boy, Bandit. Good boy," Mr. Lake said.

"This is my friend, Ricky. And this is his dad," Tom said.

"You have all helped me a lot," Mr. Lake said.

"Here is the box with your plans," Ricky said.

"We saw your plans, Mr. Lake. Bandit took the box to my house. We opened the box. I hope that was all right," Ricky said.

"That was all right to do. I think Bandit knew it would help me," Mr. Lake said.

"Mr. Lake," Tom said.

"Yes," Mr. Lake answered.

"Do you think we could see your Chocolate Machine?" Tom asked.

"Let me tell you all about that," Mr. Lake said.

Tom, Ricky, and Ricky's dad all sat down.

"I have made a lot of machines. Ten years ago I wanted to make a machine to make chocolate very fast. That man, Bill, worked for me. I told him the machine would not work." Mr Lake said.

"You mean that man we got?" Ricky said.

"That's right. Bill said it would work. But I knew it wouldn't. I put the plans away," Mr Lake said.

"What did Bill do?" Ricky asked.

"Bill got mad. He went away. Then he called me two weeks ago. He asked about the machine. I told him it didn't work. He came to town. He said he wanted the plans. I told him he couldn't have the plans," Mr. Lake said.

"Did you hide them?" Tom asked.

"No. Bandit did. Bandit did not like Bill," Mr. Lake said.

"Well, Sergeant Collins has Bill. He won't hurt you or Bandit again," Ricky said.

"Thank you for helping me and Bandit," Mr. Lake said.

"That's OK," Tom said.

"Come back again," Mr. Lake said.

"We sure will," Ricky said.

"Bring Patches with you. I think Patches and Bandit are good friends," Mr. Lake said.

"They sure are," Ricky said.

"Here. Have some chocolate."

Then Mr. Lake got another box and opened it up. "Here. Have some chocolate. It isn't from my machine, but it sure is good!"

"OK, boys. We have to get going," Ricky's dad said.

"Why is that?" Ricky said.

"I think you have some fish to clean," he said.

Patches and Bandit started to bark. They all laughed.